W9-BPR-792

DOROTHY AND THE WIZARD IN OZ

VOL. 1

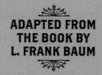

ADAPTED FROM
THE BOOK BY
L. FRANK BAUM

Writer: ERIC SHANOWER
Artist: SKOTTIE YOUNG
Colorist: JEAN-FRANCOIS BEAULIEU
Letterer: JEFF ECKLEBERRY

Assistant Editors: RACHEL PINNELAS & JON MOISAN
Editor: SANA AMANAT

Collection Editor: MARK D. BEAZLEY
Assistant Editors: NELSON RIBEIRO & ALEX STARBUCK
Editor, Special Projects: JENNIFER GRÜNWALD
Senior Editor, Special Projects: JEFF YOUNGQUIST
Senior Vice President Print, Sales & Marketing: DAVID GABRIEL

Editor in Chief: AXEL ALONSO
Chief Creative Officer: JOE QUESADA
Publisher: DAN BUCKLEY
Executive Producer: ALAN FINE

ABDO
Spotlight

MARVEL

ABDOPUBLISHING.COM

Reinforced library bound edition published in 2015 by Spotlight,
a division of ABDO, PO Box 398166, Minneapolis, Minnesota 55439.
Spotlight produces high-quality reinforced library bound editions for
schools and libraries. Published by agreement with Marvel Characters, Inc.

Printed in the United States of America, North Mankato, Minnesota.
112014
012015

THIS BOOK CONTAINS
RECYCLED MATERIALS

Marvel.com

LIBRARY OF CONGRESS CATALOGING-IN-PUBLICATION DATA

Shanower, Eric.
  Dorothy and the Wizard in Oz / adapted from the novel by L. Frank Baum ;
writer: Eric Shanower ; artist: Skottie Young. -- Reinforced library bound
edition.
     pages cm
  "Marvel."
  Summary: During a California earthquake Dorothy falls into the
underground Land of the Mangaboos where she again meets the Wizard of
Oz.
  ISBN 978-1-61479-343-4 (vol. 1) -- ISBN 978-1-61479-344-1 (vol. 2) -- ISBN
978-1-61479-345-8 (vol. 3) -- ISBN 978-1-61479-346-5 (vol. 4) -- ISBN 978-1-
61479-347-2 (vol. 5) -- ISBN 978-1-61479-348-9 (vol. 6) -- ISBN 978-1-61479-
349-6 (vol. 7) -- ISBN 978-1-61479-350-2 (vol. 8)
  1. Graphic novels. [1. Graphic novels. 2. Fantasy.] I. Young, Skottie,
illustrator. II. Baum, L. Frank (Lyman Frank), 1856-1919. Dorothy and the
Wizard in Oz. III. Title.
  PZ7.7.S453Dor 2015
  741.5'973--dc23
                          2014033625

Spotlight

A Division of ABDO
abdopublishing.com

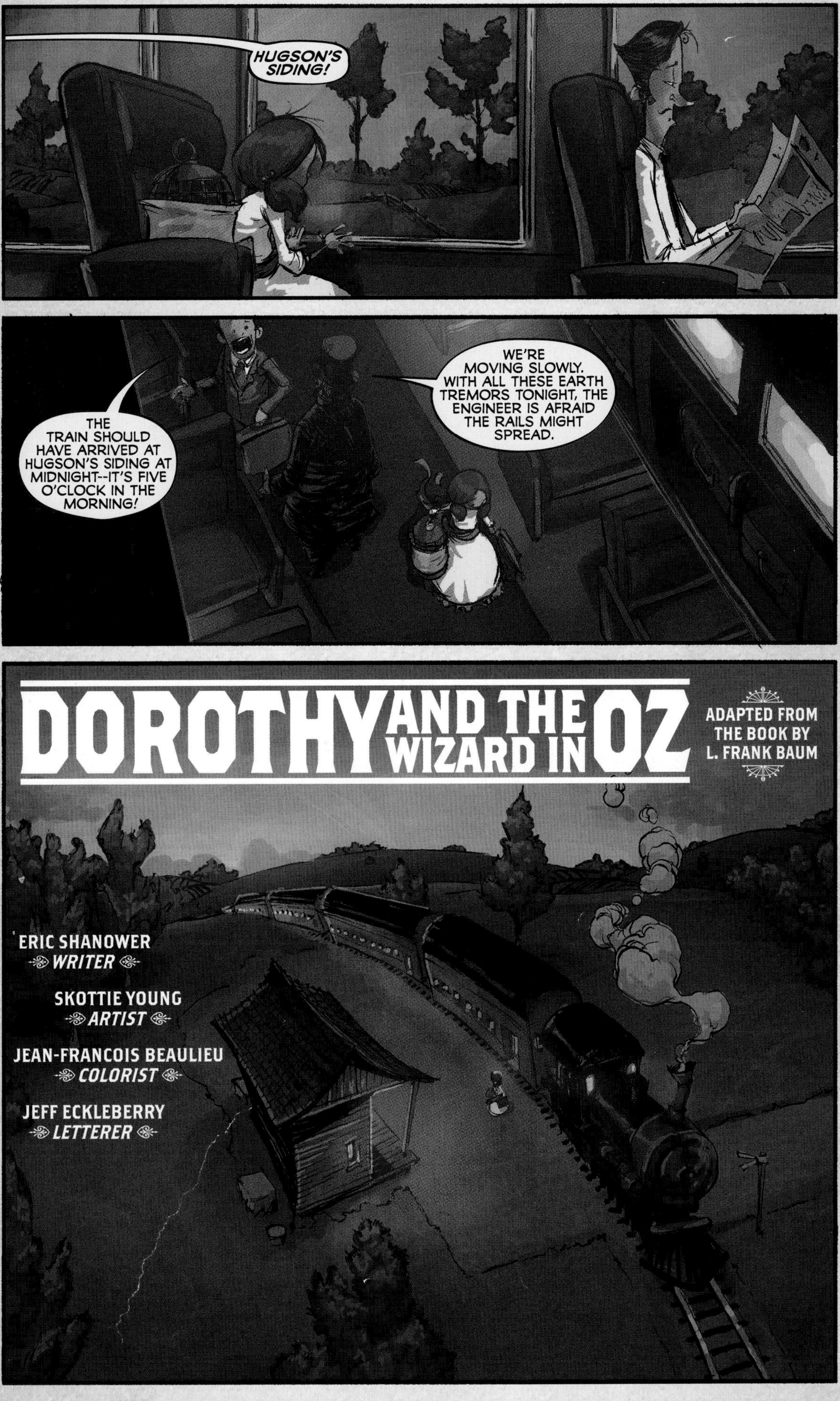
HUGSON'S SIDING!
THE TRAIN SHOULD HAVE ARRIVED AT HUGSON'S SIDING AT MIDNIGHT--IT'S FIVE O'CLOCK IN THE MORNING!
WE'RE MOVING SLOWLY. WITH ALL THESE EARTH TREMORS TONIGHT, THE ENGINEER IS AFRAID THE RAILS MIGHT SPREAD.
DOROTHY AND THE WIZARD IN OZ
ADAPTED FROM THE BOOK BY L. FRANK BAUM
ERIC SHANOWER
WRITER
SKOTTIE YOUNG
ARTIST
JEAN-FRANCOIS BEAULIEU
COLORIST
JEFF ECKLEBERRY
LETTERER

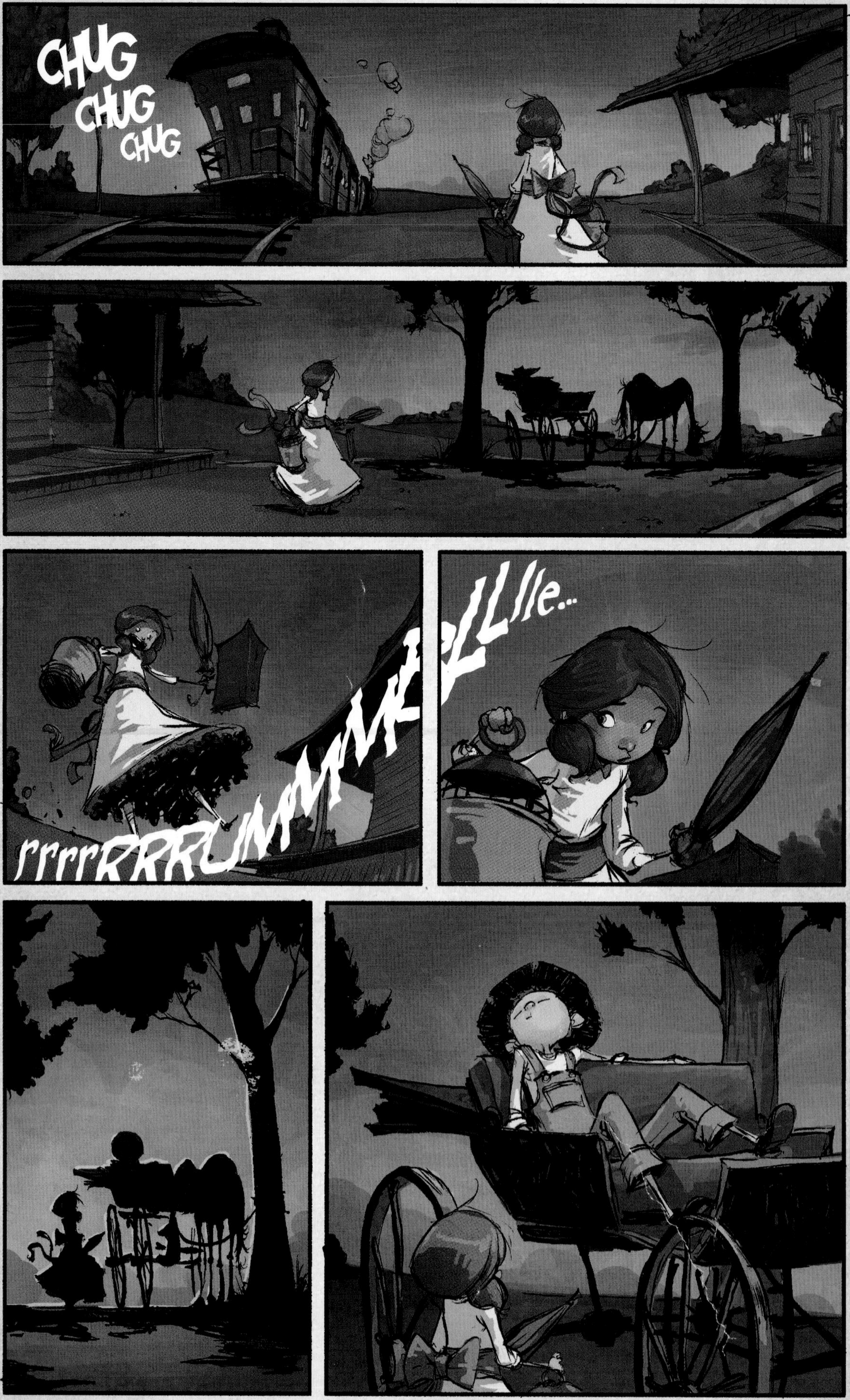
CHUG
CHUG
CHUG
rrrrRRRUMMMBLLlle...

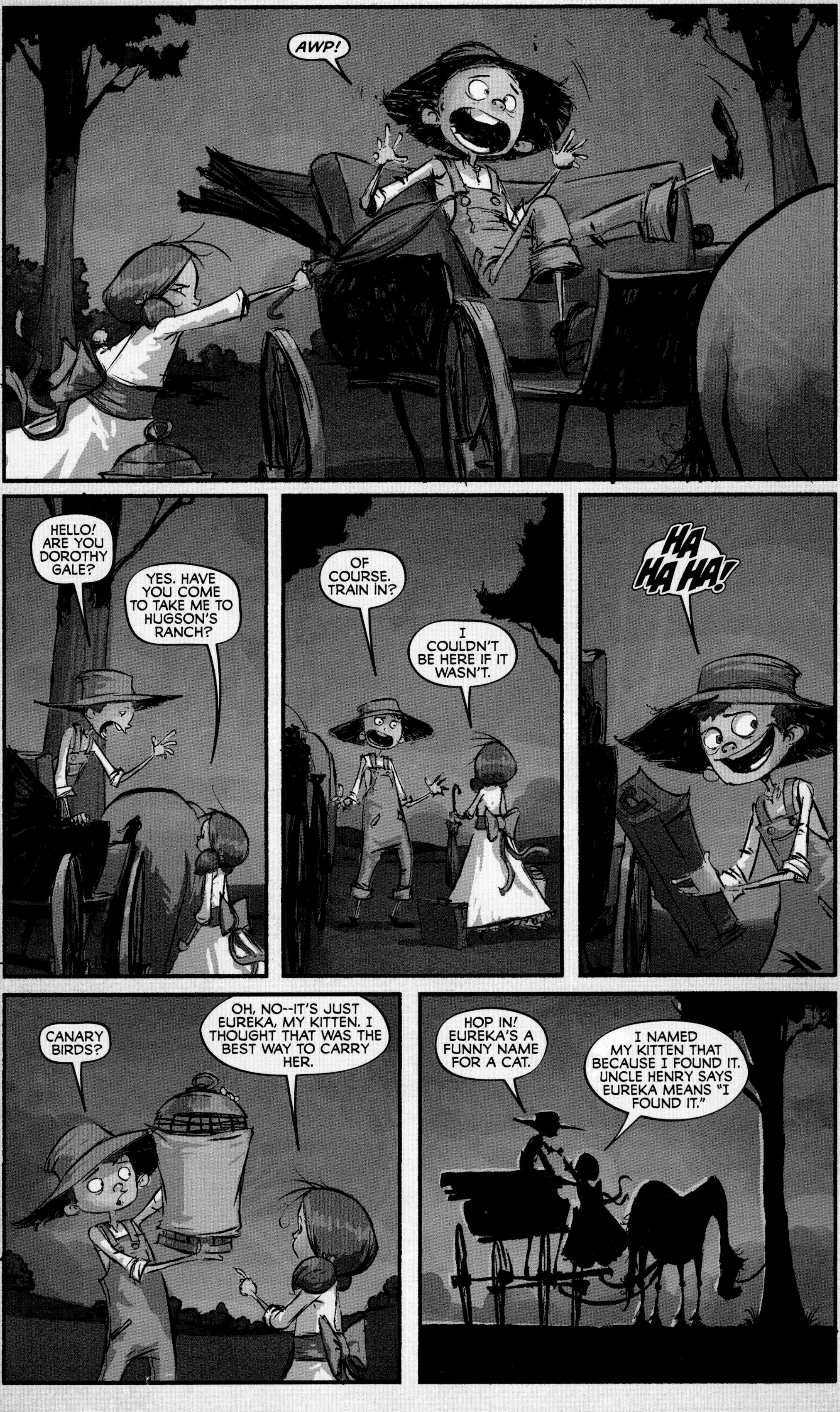
AWP!
HELLO! ARE YOU DOROTHY GALE?
YES. HAVE YOU COME TO TAKE ME TO HUGSON'S RANCH?
OF COURSE. TRAIN IN?
I COULDN'T BE HERE IF IT WASN'T.
HA HA HA!
CANARY BIRDS?
OH, NO--IT'S JUST EUREKA, MY KITTEN. I THOUGHT THAT WAS THE BEST WAY TO CARRY HER.
HOP IN! EUREKA'S A FUNNY NAME FOR A CAT.
I NAMED MY KITTEN THAT BECAUSE I FOUND IT. UNCLE HENRY SAYS EUREKA MEANS "I FOUND IT."

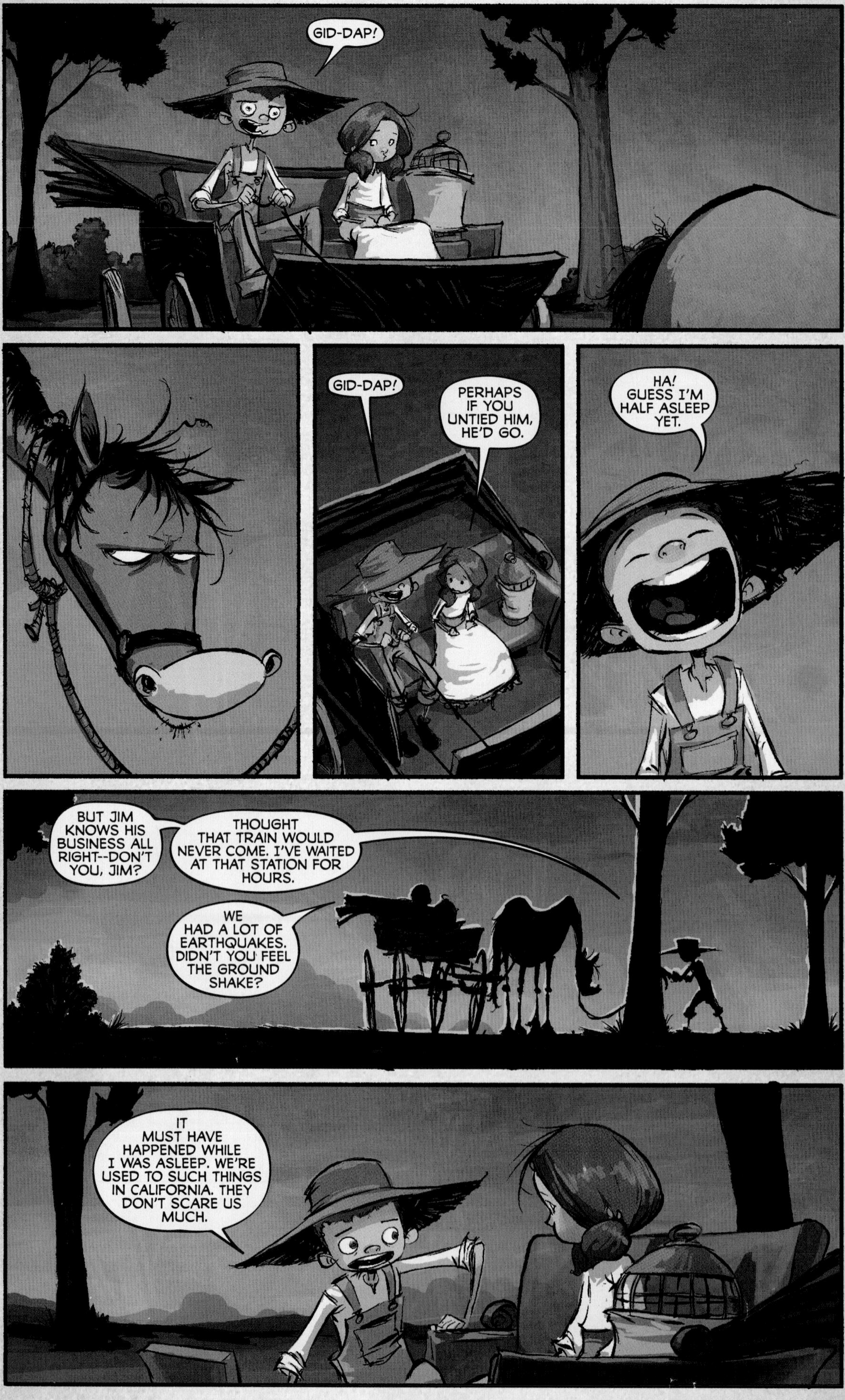
GID-DAP!
GID-DAP!
PERHAPS IF YOU UNTIED HIM, HE'D GO.
HA! GUESS I'M HALF ASLEEP YET.
THOUGHT THAT TRAIN WOULD NEVER COME. I'VE WAITED AT THAT STATION FOR HOURS.
BUT JIM KNOWS HIS BUSINESS ALL RIGHT--DON'T YOU, JIM?
WE HAD A LOT OF EARTHQUAKES. DIDN'T YOU FEEL THE GROUND SHAKE?
IT MUST HAVE HAPPENED WHILE I WAS ASLEEP. WE'RE USED TO SUCH THINGS IN CALIFORNIA. THEY DON'T SCARE US MUCH.

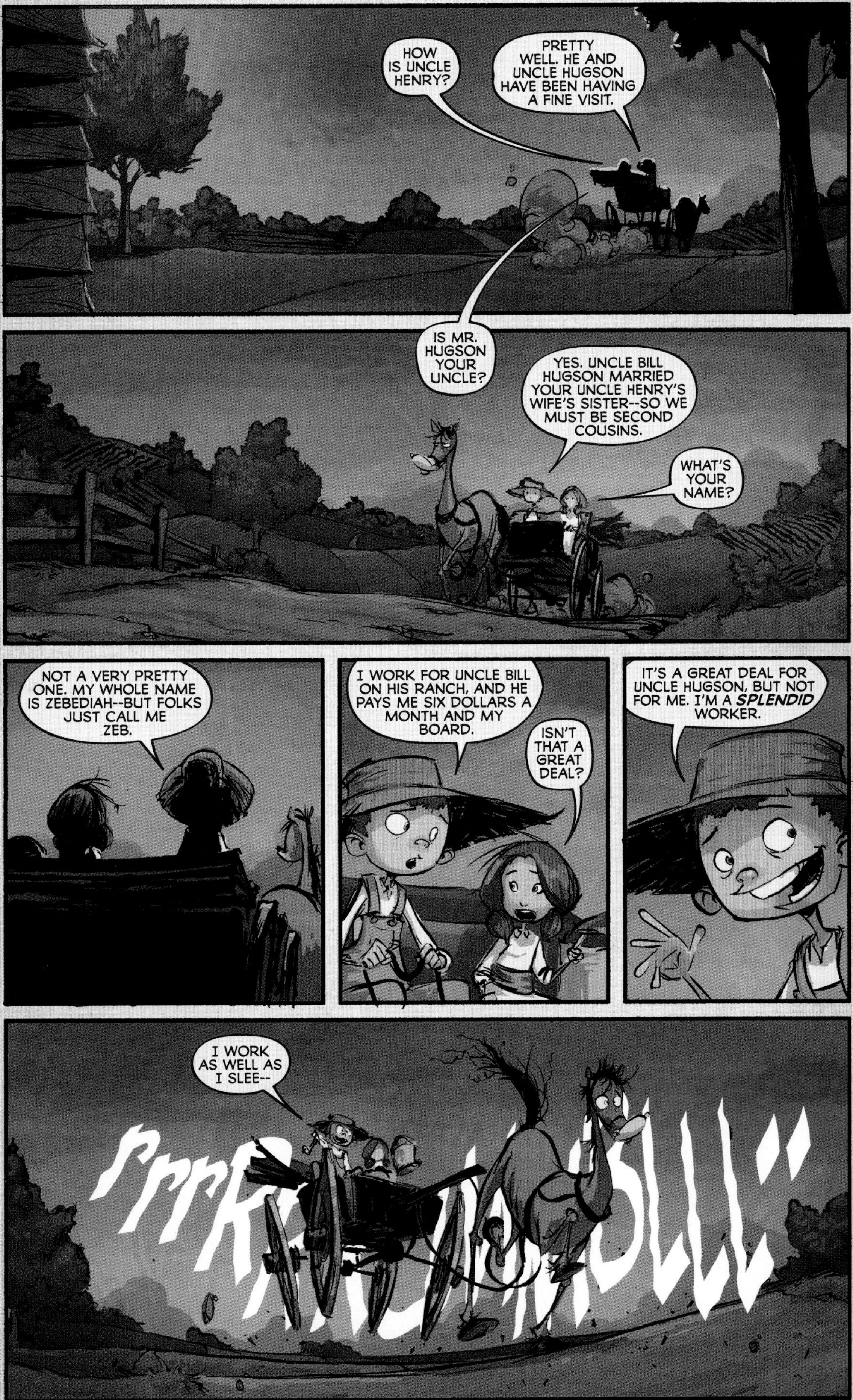
HOW IS UNCLE HENRY?
PRETTY WELL. HE AND UNCLE HUGSON HAVE BEEN HAVING A FINE VISIT.
IS MR. HUGSON YOUR UNCLE?
YES. UNCLE BILL HUGSON MARRIED YOUR UNCLE HENRY'S WIFE'S SISTER--SO WE MUST BE SECOND COUSINS.
WHAT'S YOUR NAME?
NOT A VERY PRETTY ONE. MY WHOLE NAME IS ZEBEDIAH--BUT FOLKS JUST CALL ME ZEB.
I WORK FOR UNCLE BILL ON HIS RANCH, AND HE PAYS ME SIX DOLLARS A MONTH AND MY BOARD.
ISN'T THAT A GREAT DEAL?
IT'S A GREAT DEAL FOR UNCLE HUGSON, BUT NOT FOR ME. I'M A *SPLENDID* WORKER.
I WORK AS WELL AS I SLEE--

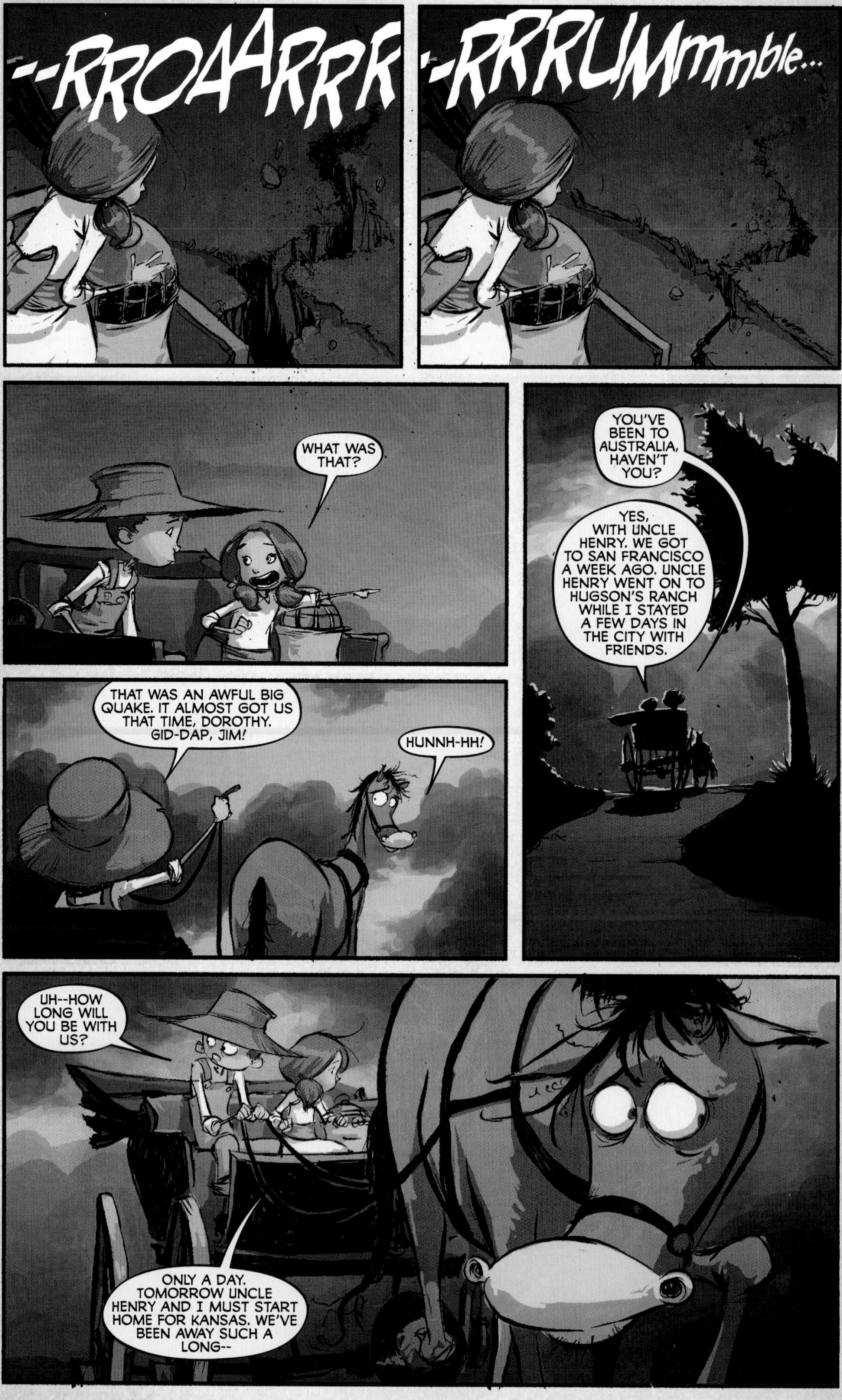
--RROAARRR
--RRRUMmmble...
WHAT WAS THAT?
THAT WAS AN AWFUL BIG QUAKE. IT ALMOST GOT US THAT TIME, DOROTHY. GID-DAP, JIM!
HUNNH-HH!
YOU'VE BEEN TO AUSTRALIA, HAVEN'T YOU?
YES, WITH UNCLE HENRY. WE GOT TO SAN FRANCISCO A WEEK AGO. UNCLE HENRY WENT ON TO HUGSON'S RANCH WHILE I STAYED A FEW DAYS IN THE CITY WITH FRIENDS.
UH--HOW LONG WILL YOU BE WITH US?
ONLY A DAY. TOMORROW UNCLE HENRY AND I MUST START HOME FOR KANSAS. WE'VE BEEN AWAY SUCH A LONG--

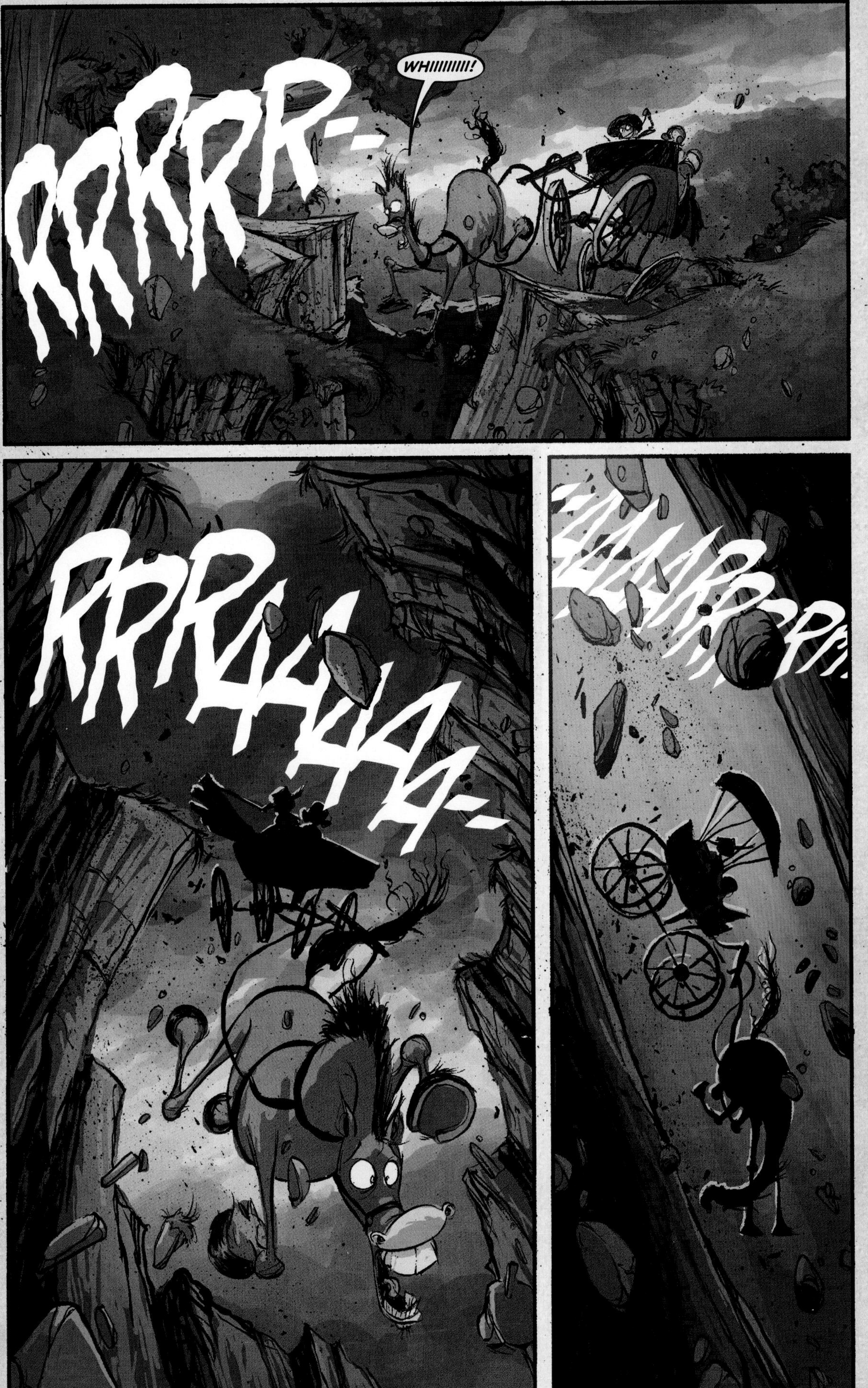
RRRRR--
WHIIIIIIIIIII!
RRRAAAA--

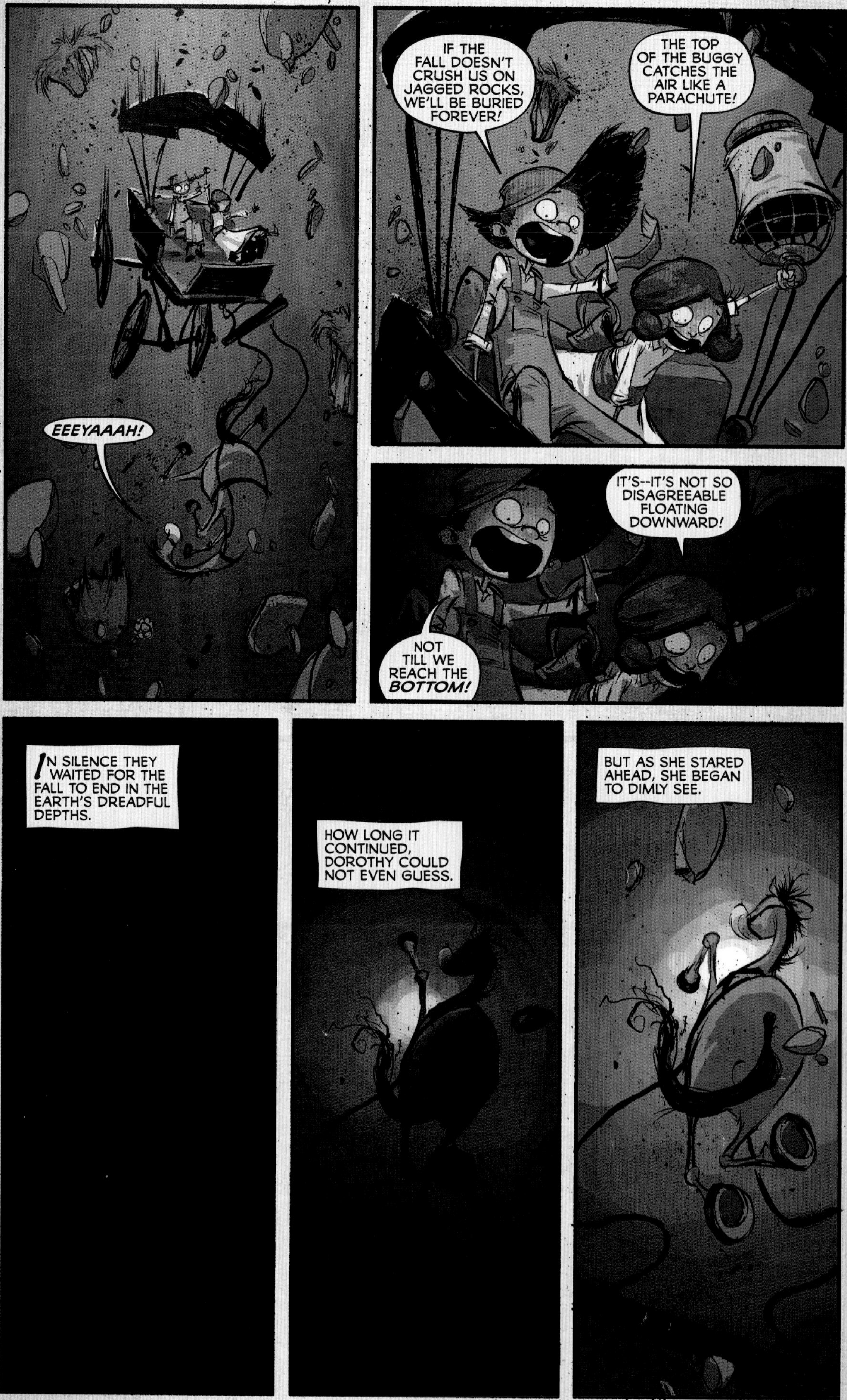
EEEYAAAH!
IF THE FALL DOESN'T CRUSH US ON JAGGED ROCKS, WE'LL BE BURIED FOREVER!
THE TOP OF THE BUGGY CATCHES THE AIR LIKE A PARACHUTE!
IT'S--IT'S NOT SO DISAGREEABLE FLOATING DOWNWARD!
NOT TILL WE REACH THE *BOTTOM!*
IN SILENCE THEY WAITED FOR THE FALL TO END IN THE EARTH'S DREADFUL DEPTHS.
HOW LONG IT CONTINUED, DOROTHY COULD NOT EVEN GUESS.
BUT AS SHE STARED AHEAD, SHE BEGAN TO DIMLY SEE.

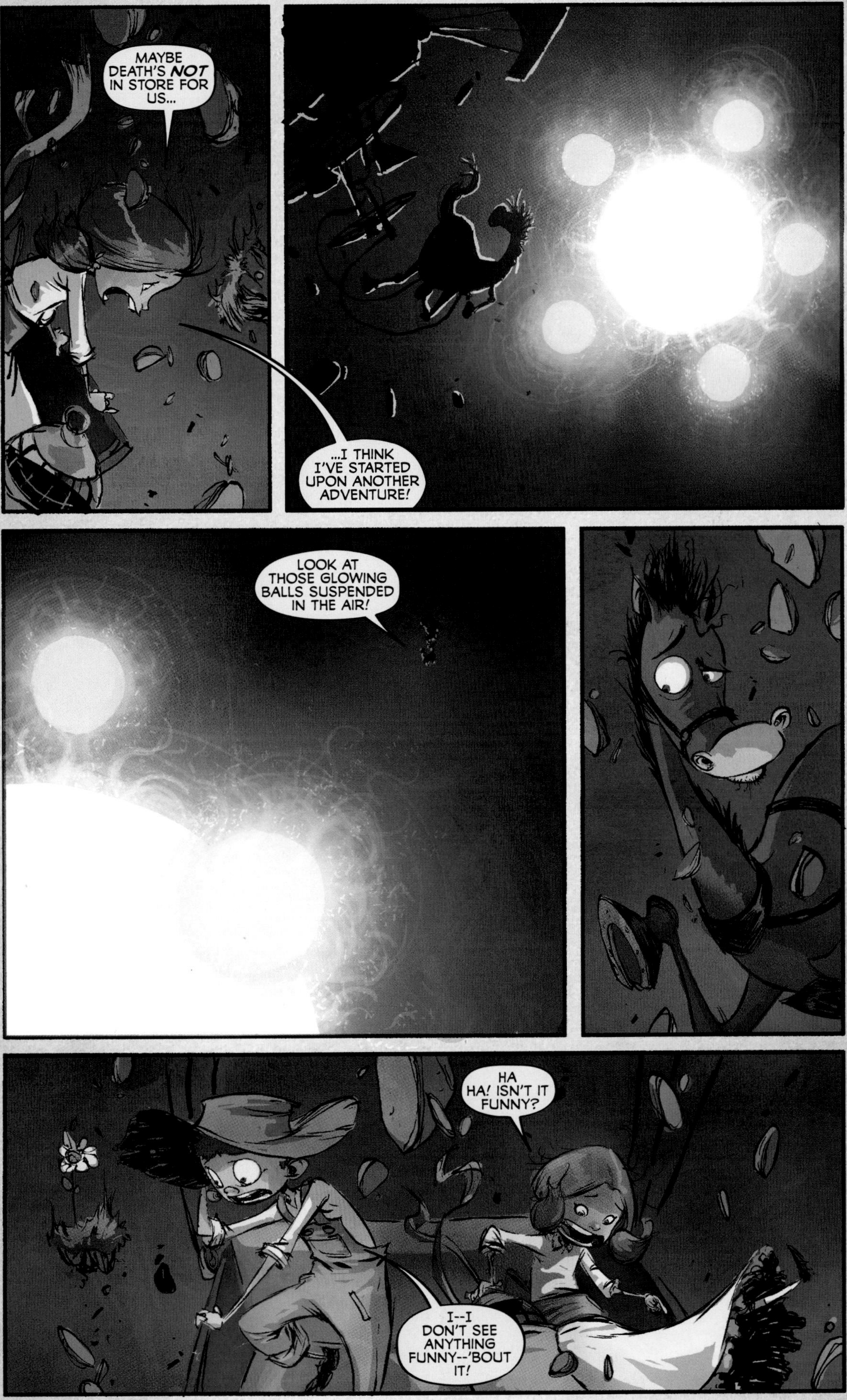
MAYBE DEATH'S *NOT* IN STORE FOR US...
...I THINK I'VE STARTED UPON ANOTHER ADVENTURE!
LOOK AT THOSE GLOWING BALLS SUSPENDED IN THE AIR!
HA HA! ISN'T IT FUNNY?
I--I DON'T SEE ANYTHING FUNNY--'BOUT IT!

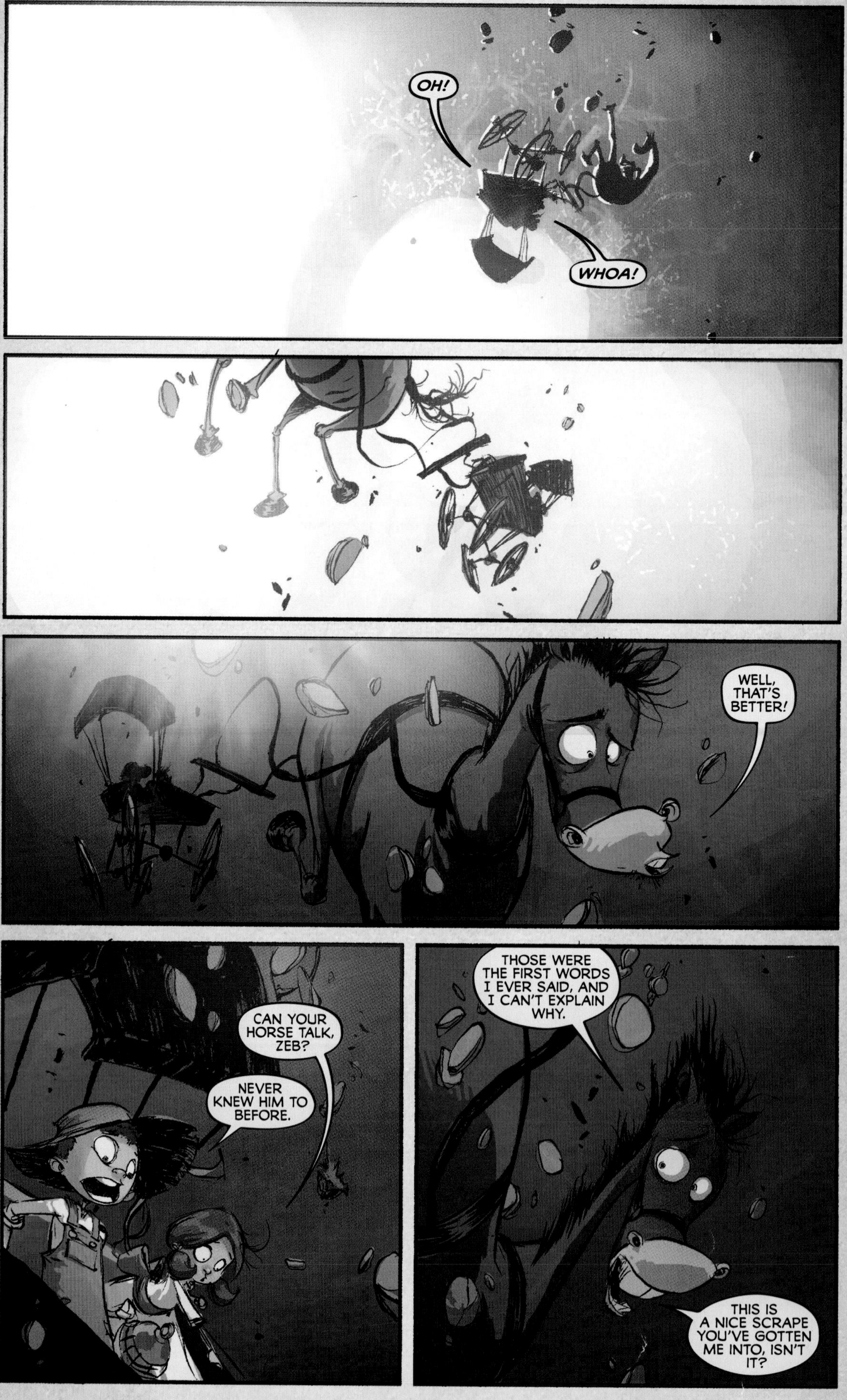
OH!
WHOA!
WELL, THAT'S BETTER!
CAN YOUR HORSE TALK, ZEB?
NEVER KNEW HIM TO BEFORE.
THOSE WERE THE FIRST WORDS I EVER SAID, AND I CAN'T EXPLAIN WHY.
THIS IS A NICE SCRAPE YOU'VE GOTTEN ME INTO, ISN'T IT?

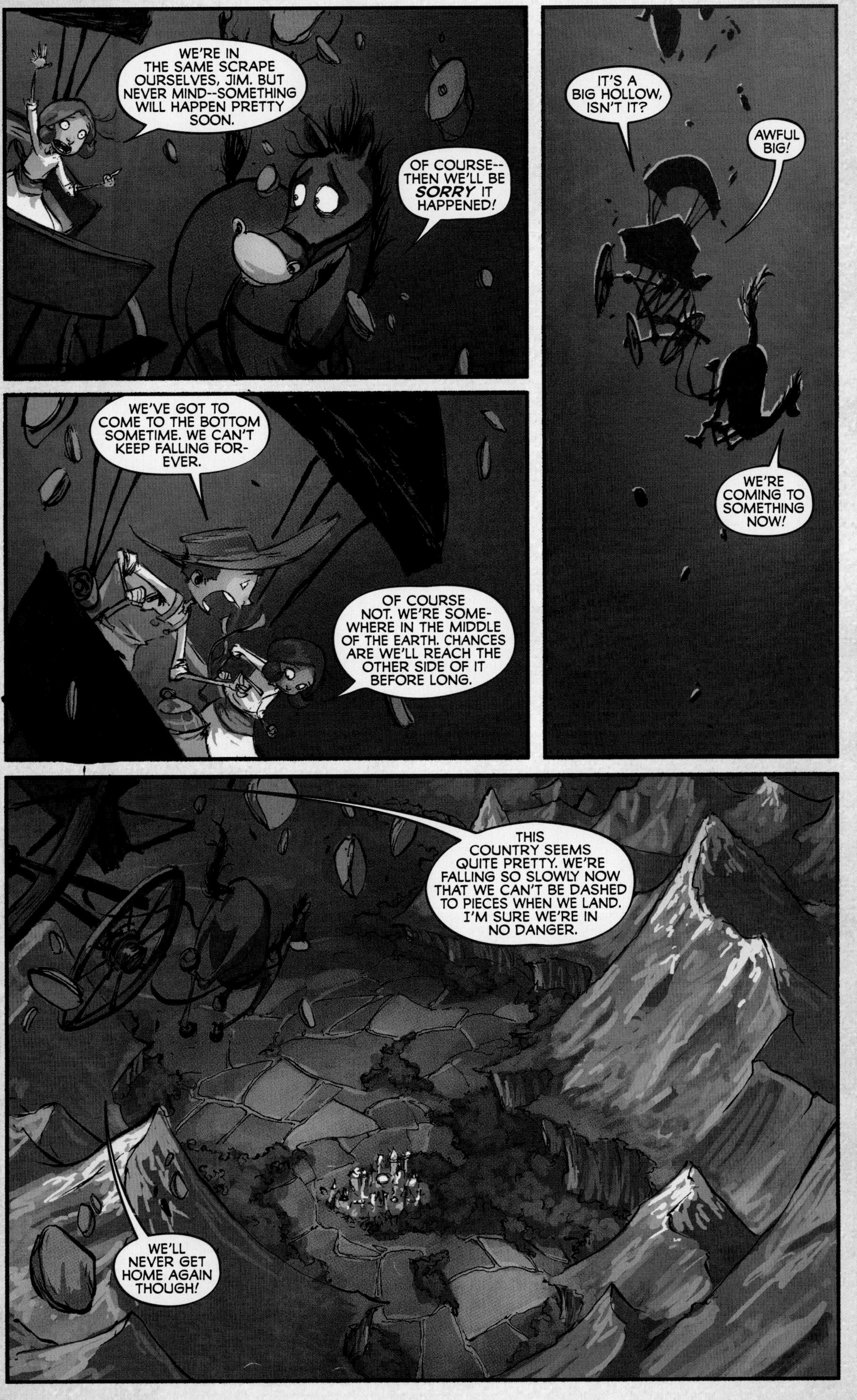
WE'RE IN THE SAME SCRAPE OURSELVES, JIM. BUT NEVER MIND--SOMETHING WILL HAPPEN PRETTY SOON.
OF COURSE--THEN WE'LL BE SORRY IT HAPPENED!
IT'S A BIG HOLLOW, ISN'T IT?
AWFUL BIG!
WE'VE GOT TO COME TO THE BOTTOM SOMETIME. WE CAN'T KEEP FALLING FOR-EVER.
OF COURSE NOT. WE'RE SOME-WHERE IN THE MIDDLE OF THE EARTH. CHANCES ARE WE'LL REACH THE OTHER SIDE OF IT BEFORE LONG.
WE'RE COMING TO SOMETHING NOW!
THIS COUNTRY SEEMS QUITE PRETTY. WE'RE FALLING SO SLOWLY NOW THAT WE CAN'T BE DASHED TO PIECES WHEN WE LAND. I'M SURE WE'RE IN NO DANGER.
WE'LL NEVER GET HOME AGAIN THOUGH!

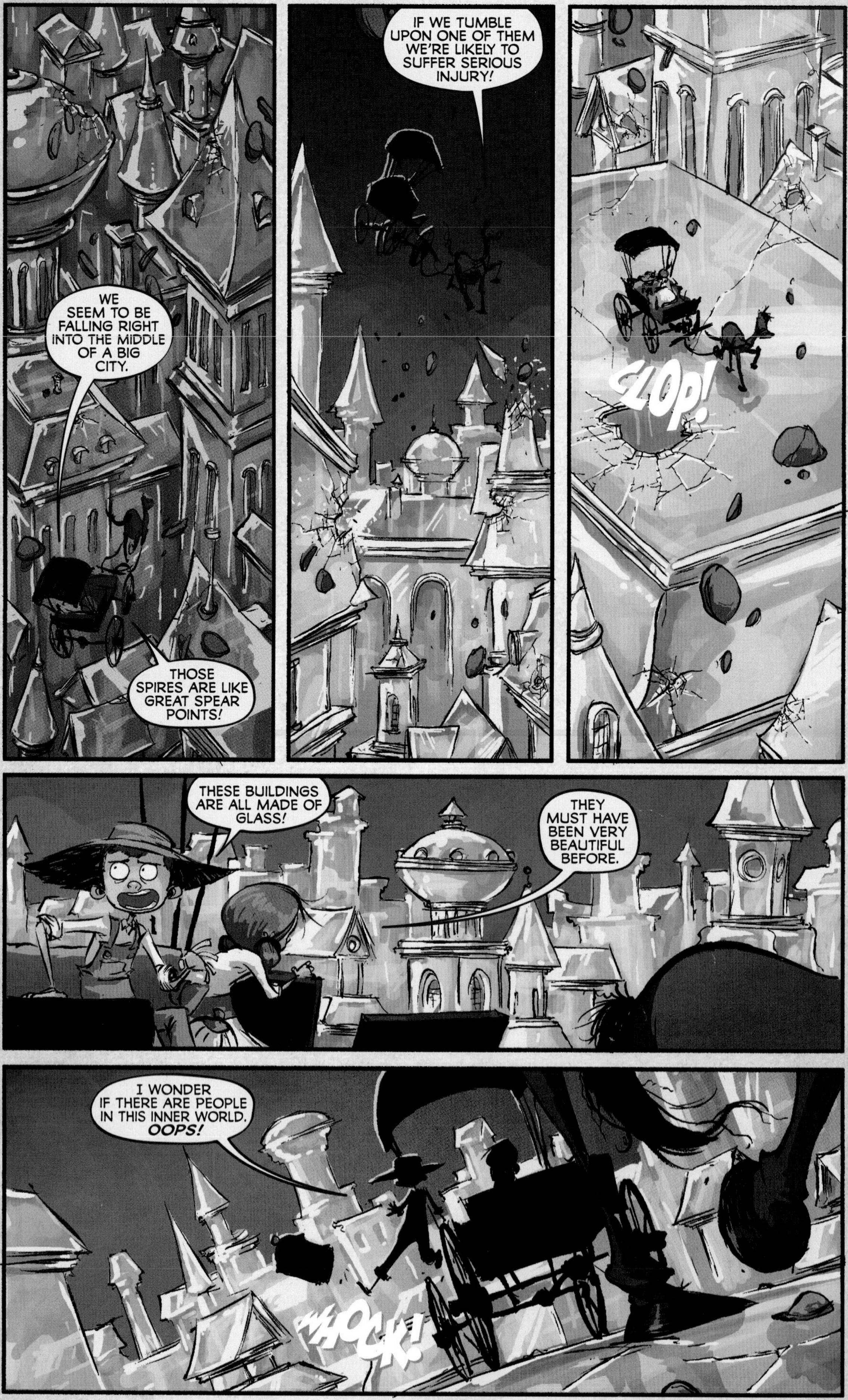
WE SEEM TO BE FALLING RIGHT INTO THE MIDDLE OF A BIG CITY.
THOSE SPIRES ARE LIKE GREAT SPEAR POINTS!
IF WE TUMBLE UPON ONE OF THEM WE'RE LIKELY TO SUFFER SERIOUS INJURY!
CLOP!
THESE BUILDINGS ARE ALL MADE OF GLASS!
THEY MUST HAVE BEEN VERY BEAUTIFUL BEFORE.
I WONDER IF THERE ARE PEOPLE IN THIS INNER WORLD. OOPS!
WHOCK!

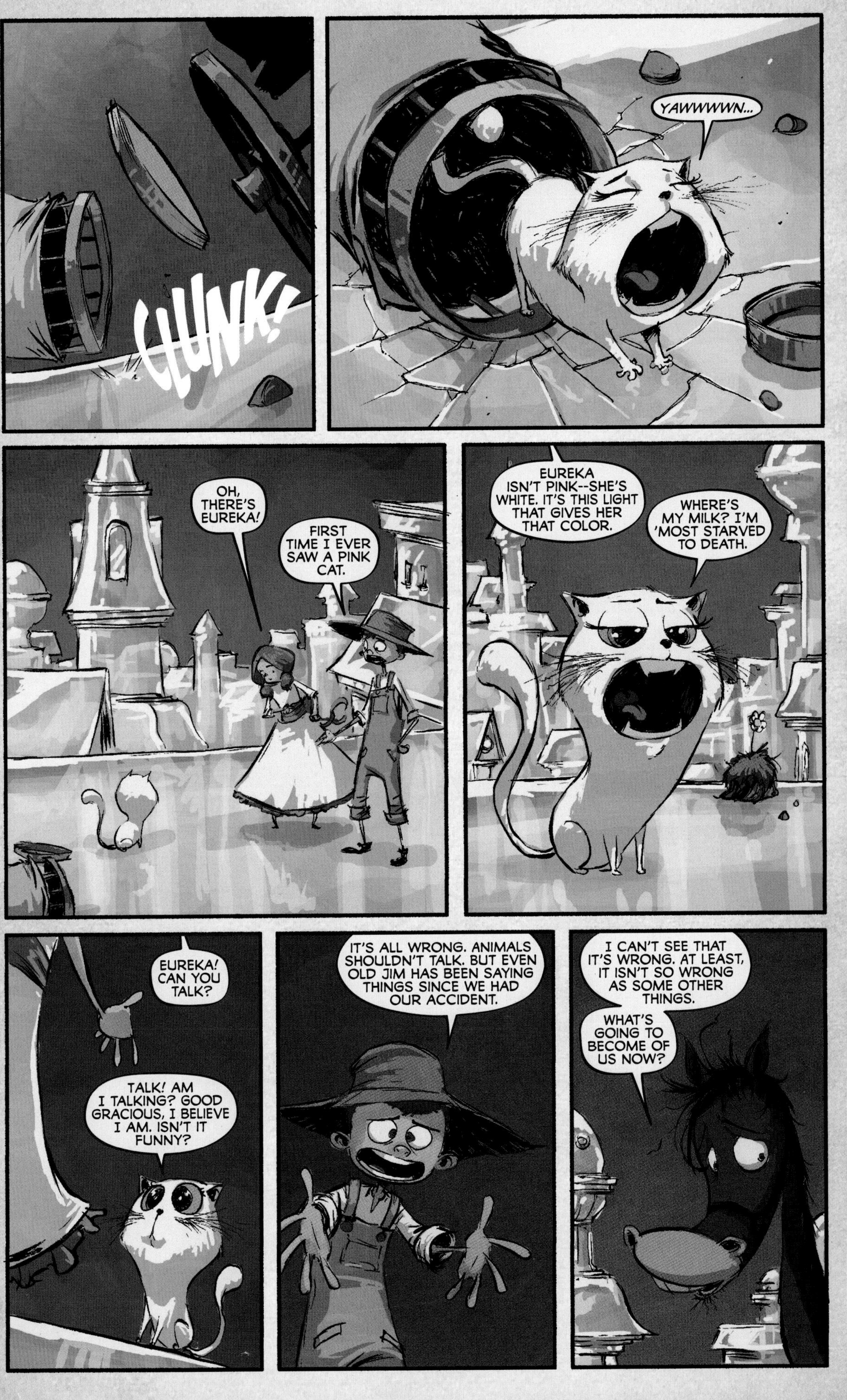
CLUNK!
YAWWWWN...
OH, THERE'S EUREKA!
FIRST TIME I EVER SAW A PINK CAT.
EUREKA ISN'T PINK--SHE'S WHITE. IT'S THIS LIGHT THAT GIVES HER THAT COLOR.
WHERE'S MY MILK? I'M 'MOST STARVED TO DEATH.
EUREKA! CAN YOU TALK?
TALK! AM I TALKING? GOOD GRACIOUS, I BELIEVE I AM. ISN'T IT FUNNY?
IT'S ALL WRONG. ANIMALS SHOULDN'T TALK. BUT EVEN OLD JIM HAS BEEN SAYING THINGS SINCE WE HAD OUR ACCIDENT.
I CAN'T SEE THAT IT'S WRONG. AT LEAST, IT ISN'T SO WRONG AS SOME OTHER THINGS.
WHAT'S GOING TO BECOME OF US NOW?

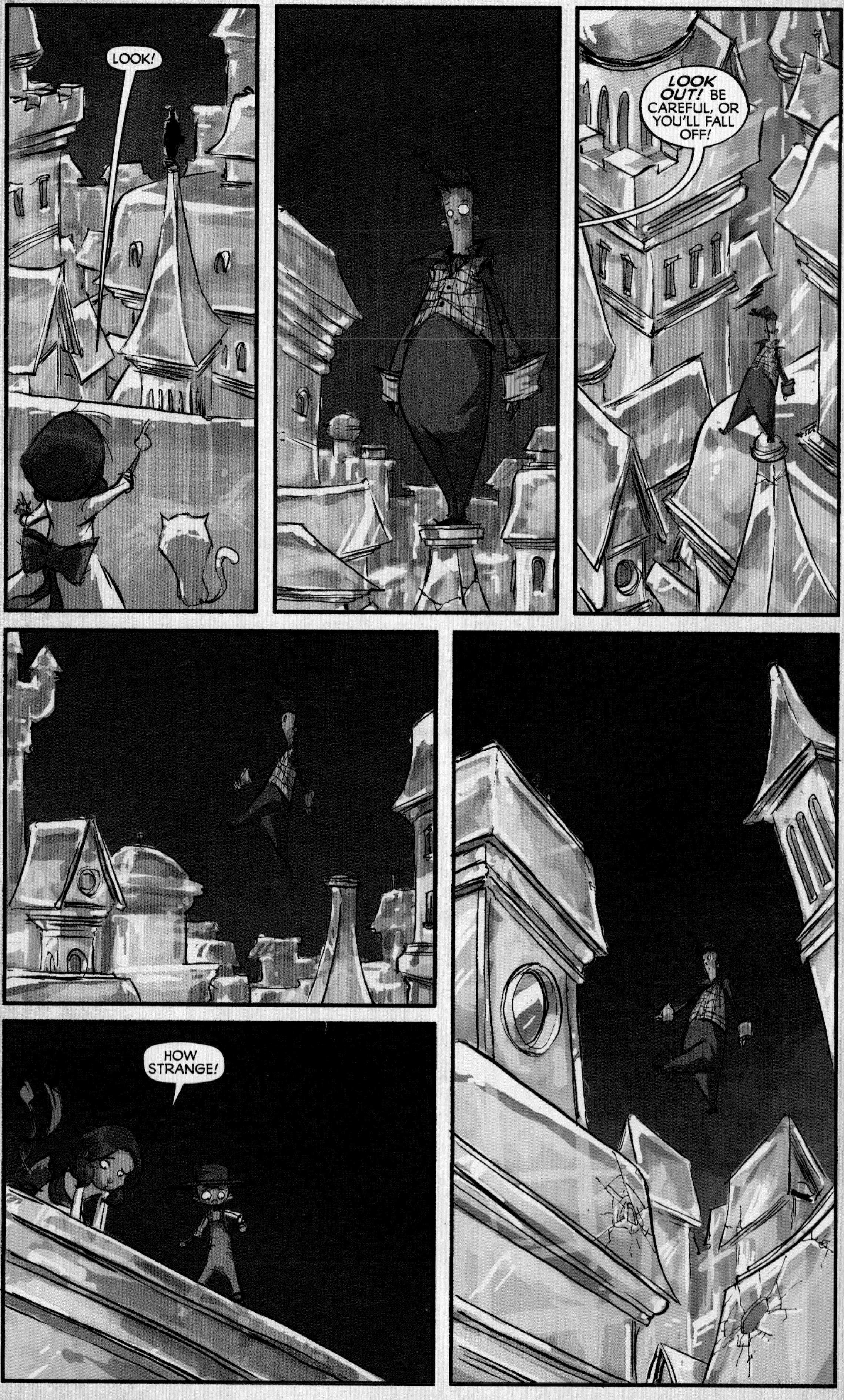
LOOK!
LOOK OUT! BE CAREFUL, OR YOU'LL FALL OFF!
HOW STRANGE!

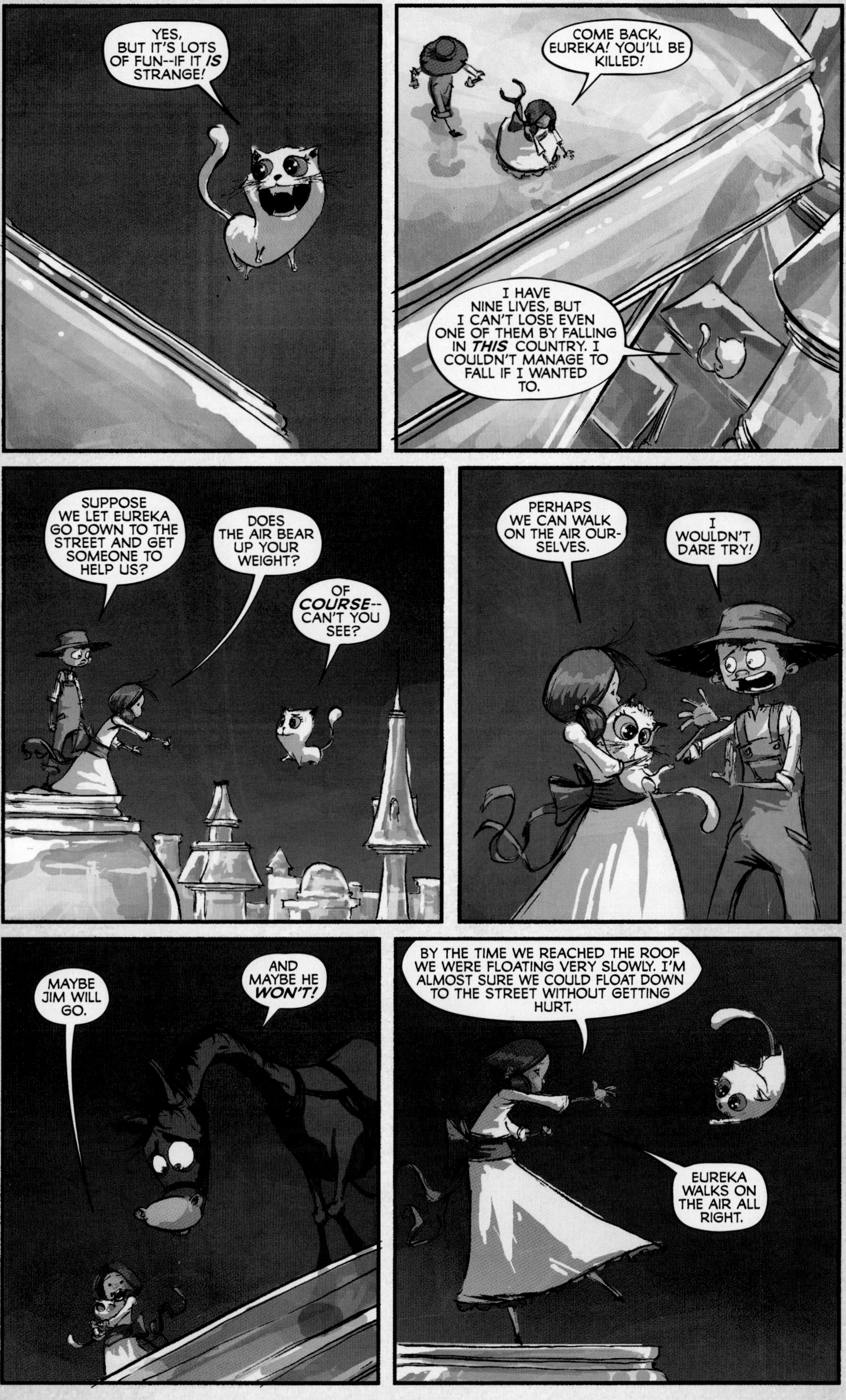
YES, BUT IT'S LOTS OF FUN--IF IT *IS* STRANGE!
COME BACK, EUREKA! YOU'LL BE KILLED!
I HAVE NINE LIVES, BUT I CAN'T LOSE EVEN ONE OF THEM BY FALLING IN *THIS* COUNTRY. I COULDN'T MANAGE TO FALL IF I WANTED TO.
SUPPOSE WE LET EUREKA GO DOWN TO THE STREET AND GET SOMEONE TO HELP US?
DOES THE AIR BEAR UP YOUR WEIGHT?
OF *COURSE*--CAN'T YOU SEE?
PERHAPS WE CAN WALK ON THE AIR OURSELVES.
I WOULDN'T DARE TRY!
MAYBE JIM WILL GO.
AND MAYBE HE *WON'T!*
BY THE TIME WE REACHED THE ROOF WE WERE FLOATING VERY SLOWLY. I'M ALMOST SURE WE COULD FLOAT DOWN TO THE STREET WITHOUT GETTING HURT.
EUREKA WALKS ON THE AIR ALL RIGHT.

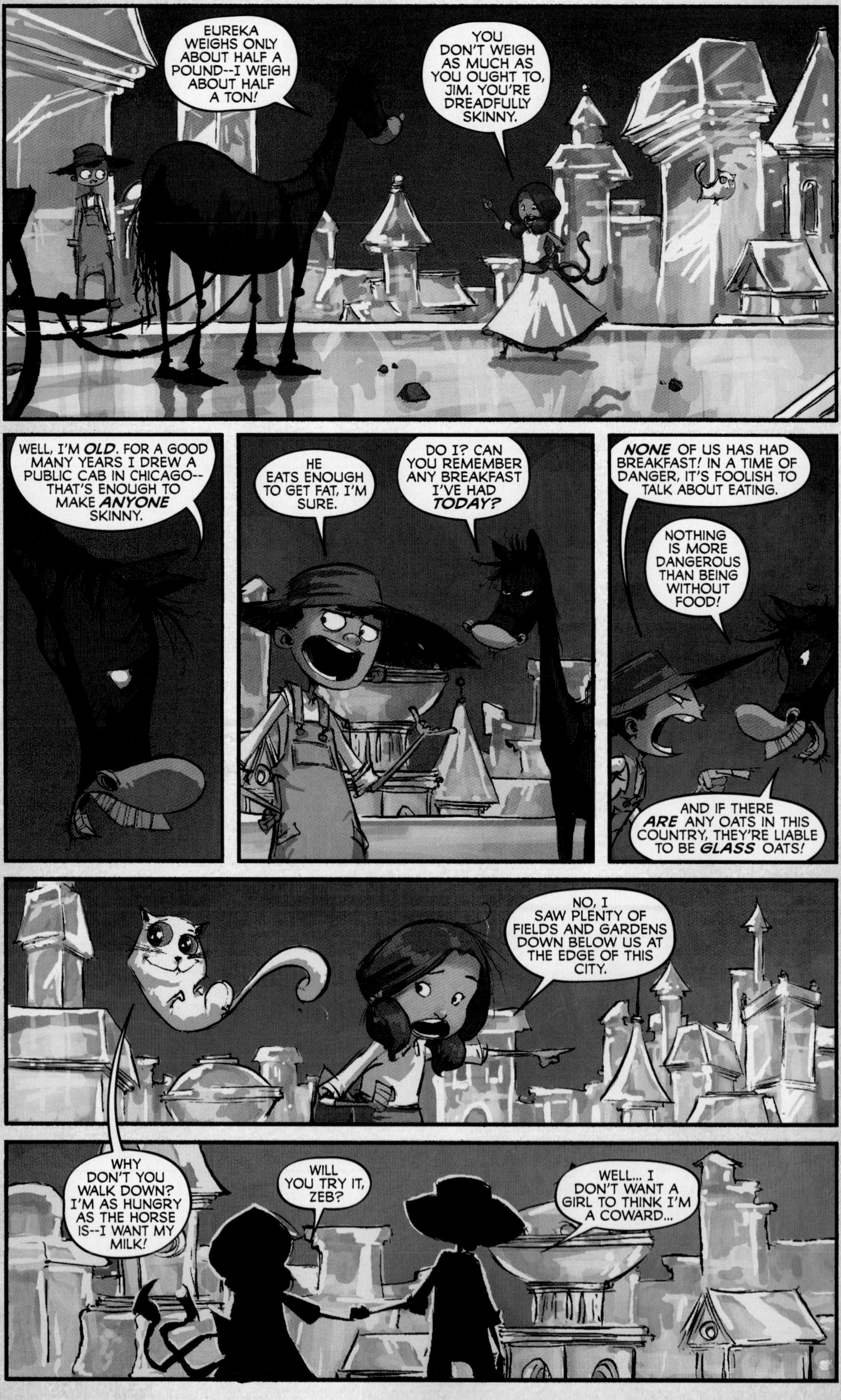
EUREKA WEIGHS ONLY ABOUT HALF A POUND--I WEIGH ABOUT HALF A TON!
YOU DON'T WEIGH AS MUCH AS YOU OUGHT TO, JIM. YOU'RE DREADFULLY SKINNY.
WELL, I'M OLD. FOR A GOOD MANY YEARS I DREW A PUBLIC CAB IN CHICAGO--THAT'S ENOUGH TO MAKE ANYONE SKINNY.
HE EATS ENOUGH TO GET FAT, I'M SURE.
DO I? CAN YOU REMEMBER ANY BREAKFAST I'VE HAD TODAY?
NONE OF US HAS HAD BREAKFAST! IN A TIME OF DANGER, IT'S FOOLISH TO TALK ABOUT EATING.
NOTHING IS MORE DANGEROUS THAN BEING WITHOUT FOOD!
AND IF THERE ARE ANY OATS IN THIS COUNTRY, THEY'RE LIABLE TO BE GLASS OATS!
NO, I SAW PLENTY OF FIELDS AND GARDENS DOWN BELOW US AT THE EDGE OF THIS CITY.
WHY DON'T YOU WALK DOWN? I'M AS HUNGRY AS THE HORSE IS--I WANT MY MILK!
WILL YOU TRY IT, ZEB?
WELL... I DON'T WANT A GIRL TO THINK I'M A COWARD...

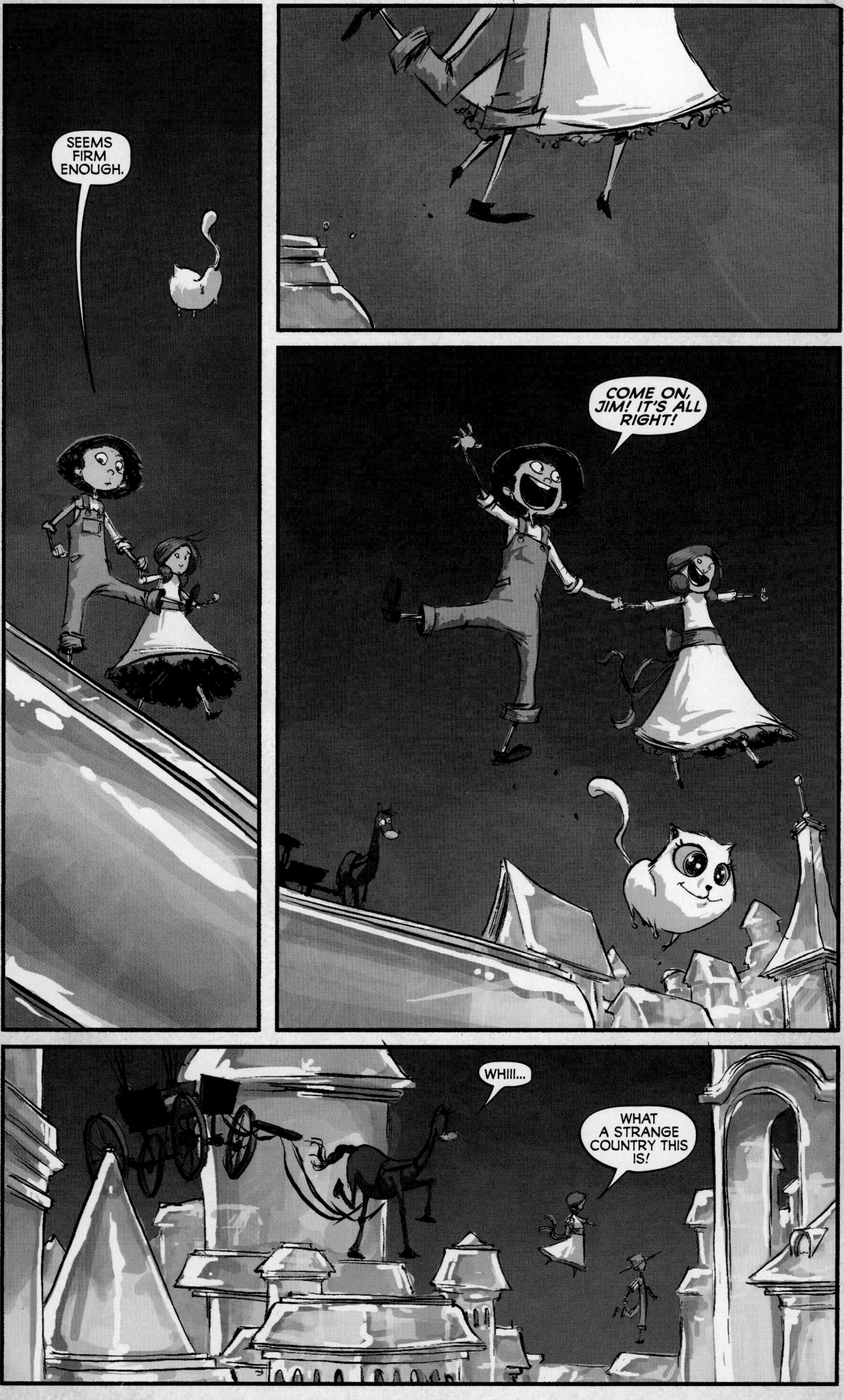
SEEMS FIRM ENOUGH.
COME ON, JIM! IT'S ALL RIGHT!
WHIII...
WHAT A STRANGE COUNTRY THIS IS!

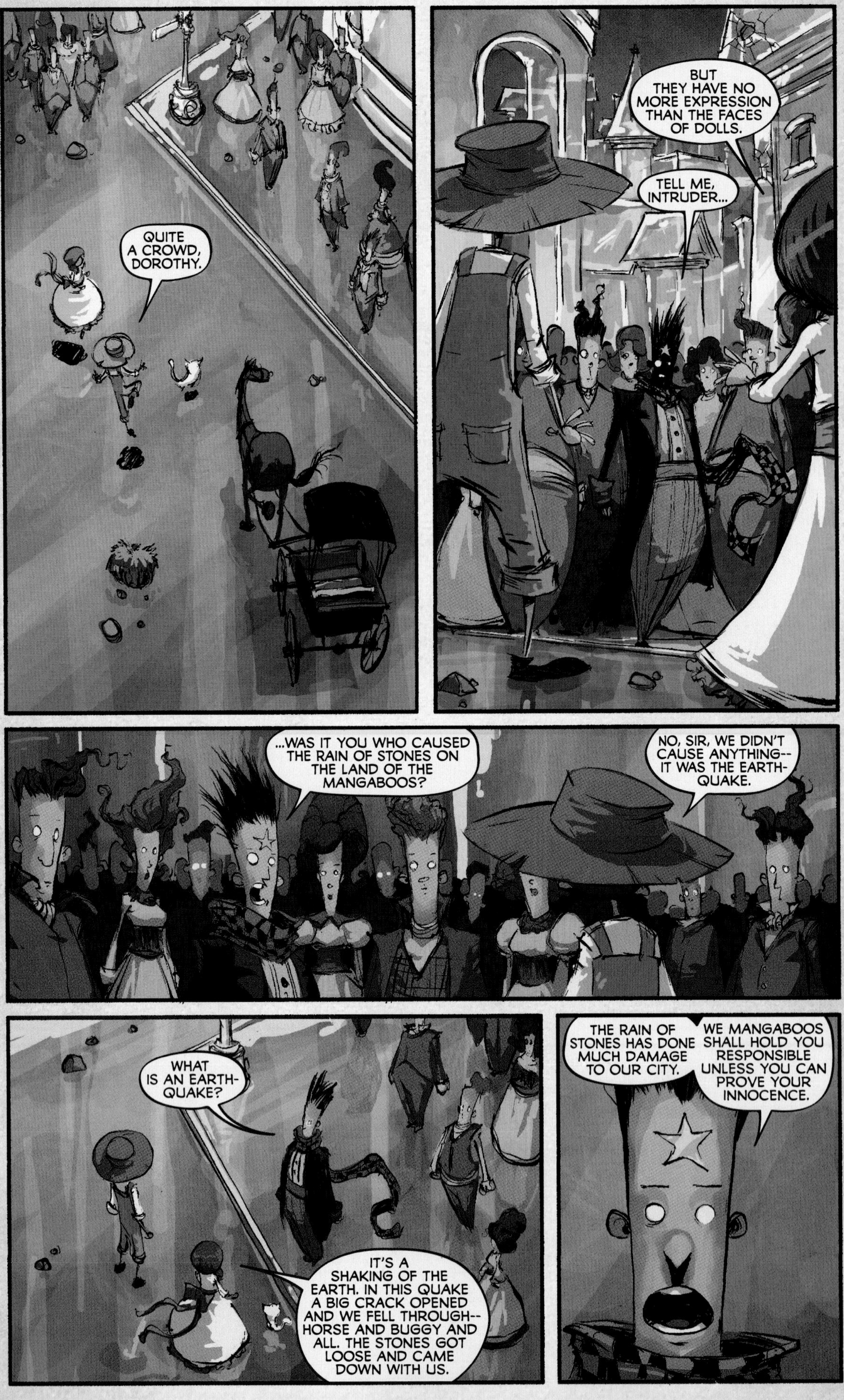
QUITE A CROWD, DOROTHY.
BUT THEY HAVE NO MORE EXPRESSION THAN THE FACES OF DOLLS.
TELL ME, INTRUDER...
...WAS IT YOU WHO CAUSED THE RAIN OF STONES ON THE LAND OF THE MANGABOOS?
NO, SIR, WE DIDN'T CAUSE ANYTHING-- IT WAS THE EARTH-QUAKE.
WHAT IS AN EARTH-QUAKE?
IT'S A SHAKING OF THE EARTH. IN THIS QUAKE A BIG CRACK OPENED AND WE FELL THROUGH-- HORSE AND BUGGY AND ALL. THE STONES GOT LOOSE AND CAME DOWN WITH US.
THE RAIN OF STONES HAS DONE MUCH DAMAGE TO OUR CITY.
WE MANGABOOS SHALL HOLD YOU RESPONSIBLE UNLESS YOU CAN PROVE YOUR INNOCENCE.

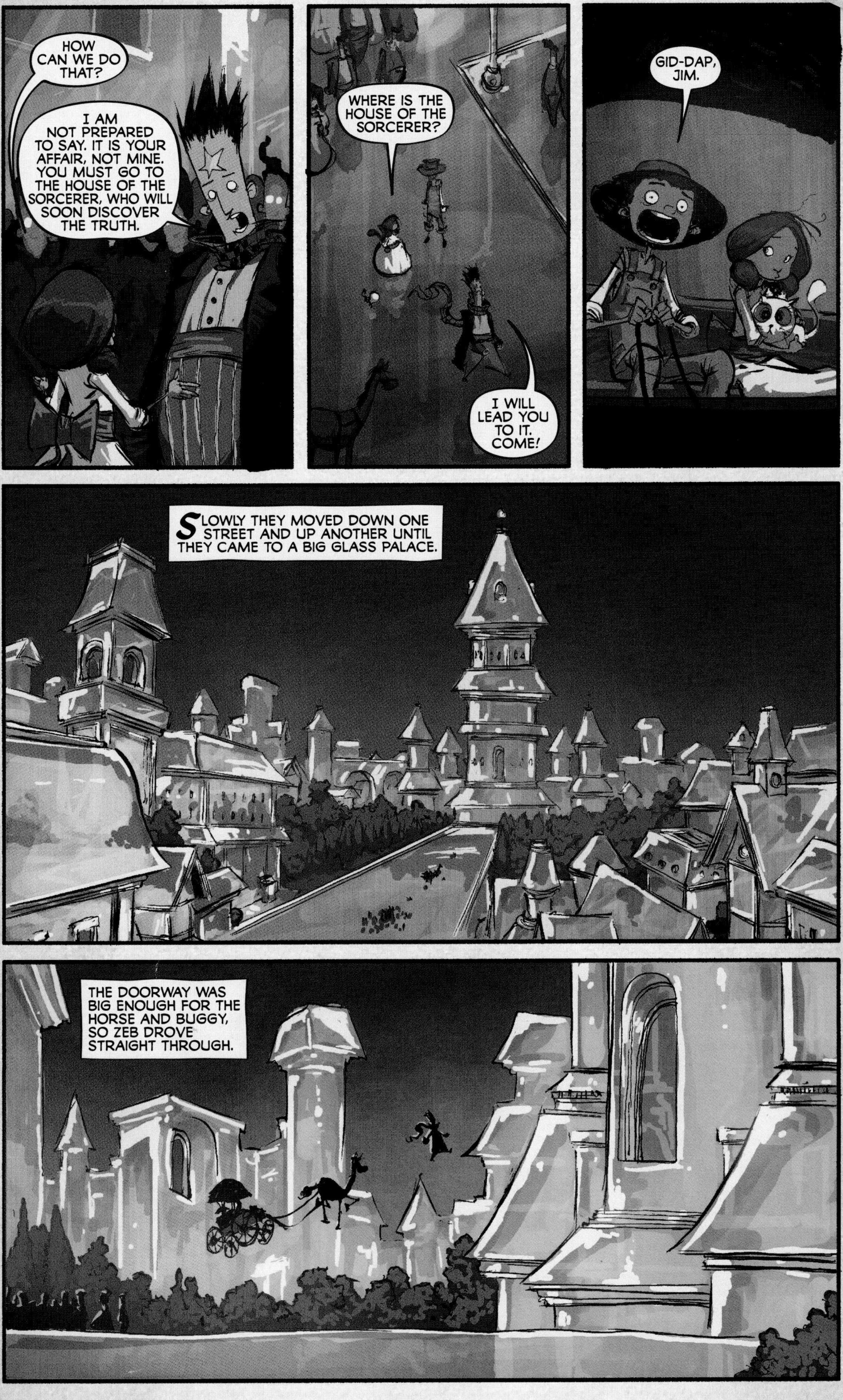
HOW CAN WE DO THAT?
I AM NOT PREPARED TO SAY. IT IS YOUR AFFAIR, NOT MINE. YOU MUST GO TO THE HOUSE OF THE SORCERER, WHO WILL SOON DISCOVER THE TRUTH.
WHERE IS THE HOUSE OF THE SORCERER?
I WILL LEAD YOU TO IT. COME!
GID-DAP, JIM.
SLOWLY THEY MOVED DOWN ONE STREET AND UP ANOTHER UNTIL THEY CAME TO A BIG GLASS PALACE.
THE DOORWAY WAS BIG ENOUGH FOR THE HORSE AND BUGGY, SO ZEB DROVE STRAIGHT THROUGH.

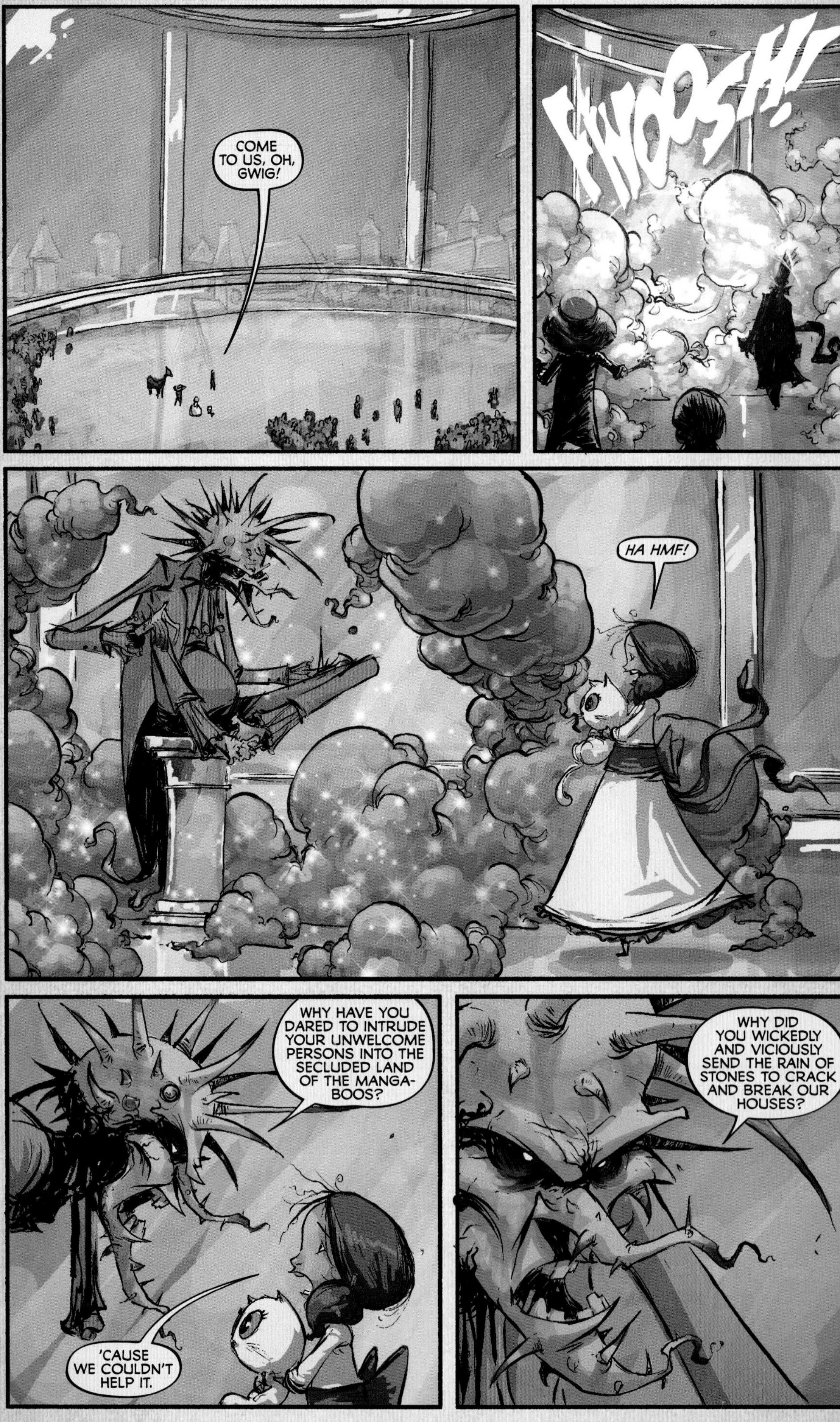
COME TO US, OH, GWIG!
FWOOSH!
HA HMF!
WHY HAVE YOU DARED TO INTRUDE YOUR UNWELCOME PERSONS INTO THE SECLUDED LAND OF THE MANGA-BOOS?
'CAUSE WE COULDN'T HELP IT.
WHY DID YOU WICKEDLY AND VICIOUSLY SEND THE RAIN OF STONES TO CRACK AND BREAK OUR HOUSES?

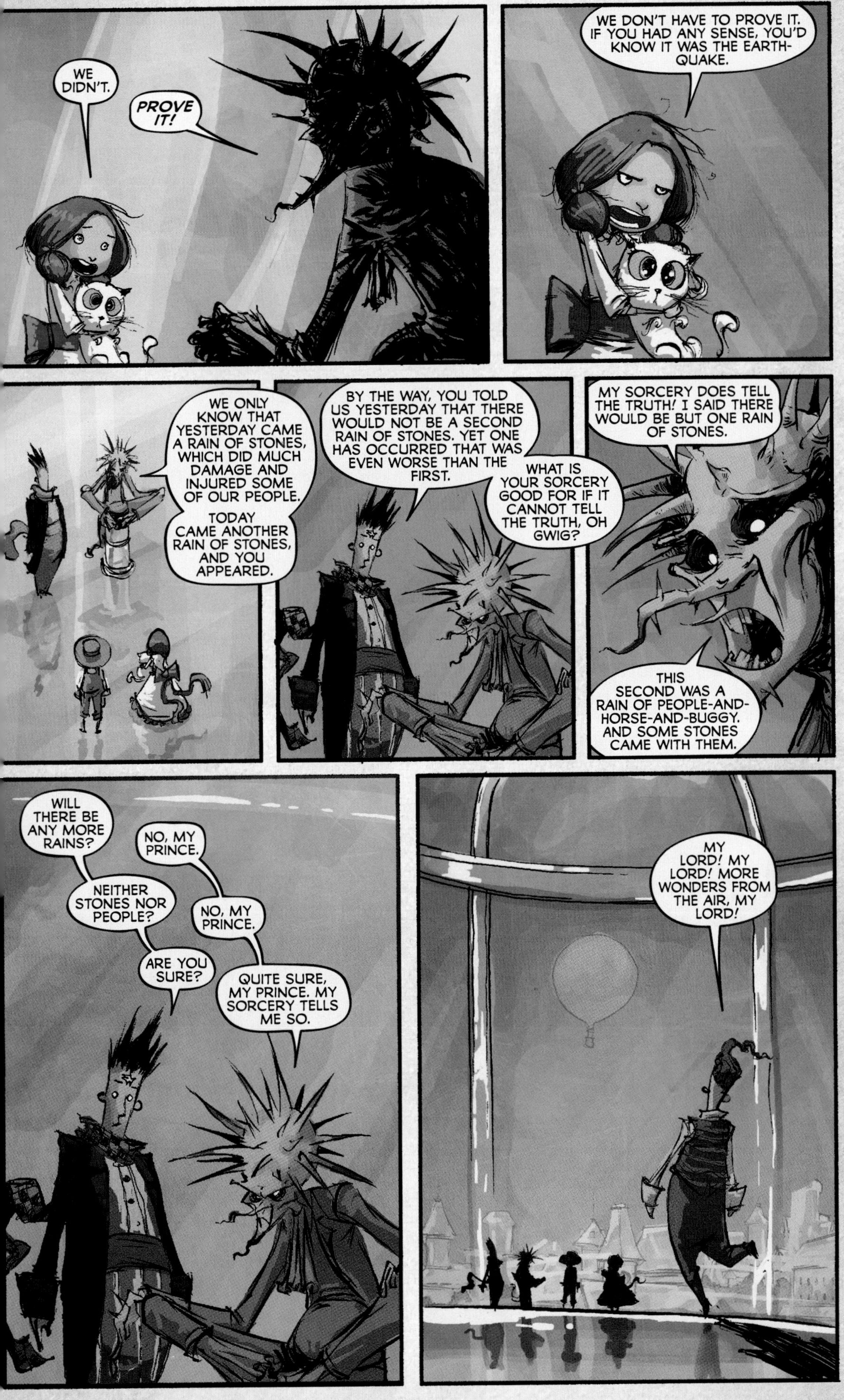
WE DIDN'T.
PROVE IT!
WE DON'T HAVE TO PROVE IT. IF YOU HAD ANY SENSE, YOU'D KNOW IT WAS THE EARTH-QUAKE.
WE ONLY KNOW THAT YESTERDAY CAME A RAIN OF STONES, WHICH DID MUCH DAMAGE AND INJURED SOME OF OUR PEOPLE.
TODAY CAME ANOTHER RAIN OF STONES, AND YOU APPEARED.
BY THE WAY, YOU TOLD US YESTERDAY THAT THERE WOULD NOT BE A SECOND RAIN OF STONES. YET ONE HAS OCCURRED THAT WAS EVEN WORSE THAN THE FIRST.
WHAT IS YOUR SORCERY GOOD FOR IF IT CANNOT TELL THE TRUTH, OH GWIG?
MY SORCERY DOES TELL THE TRUTH! I SAID THERE WOULD BE BUT ONE RAIN OF STONES.
THIS SECOND WAS A RAIN OF PEOPLE-AND-HORSE-AND-BUGGY. AND SOME STONES CAME WITH THEM.
WILL THERE BE ANY MORE RAINS?
NO, MY PRINCE.
NEITHER STONES NOR PEOPLE?
NO, MY PRINCE.
ARE YOU SURE?
QUITE SURE, MY PRINCE. MY SORCERY TELLS ME SO.
MY LORD! MY LORD! MORE WONDERS FROM THE AIR, MY LORD!

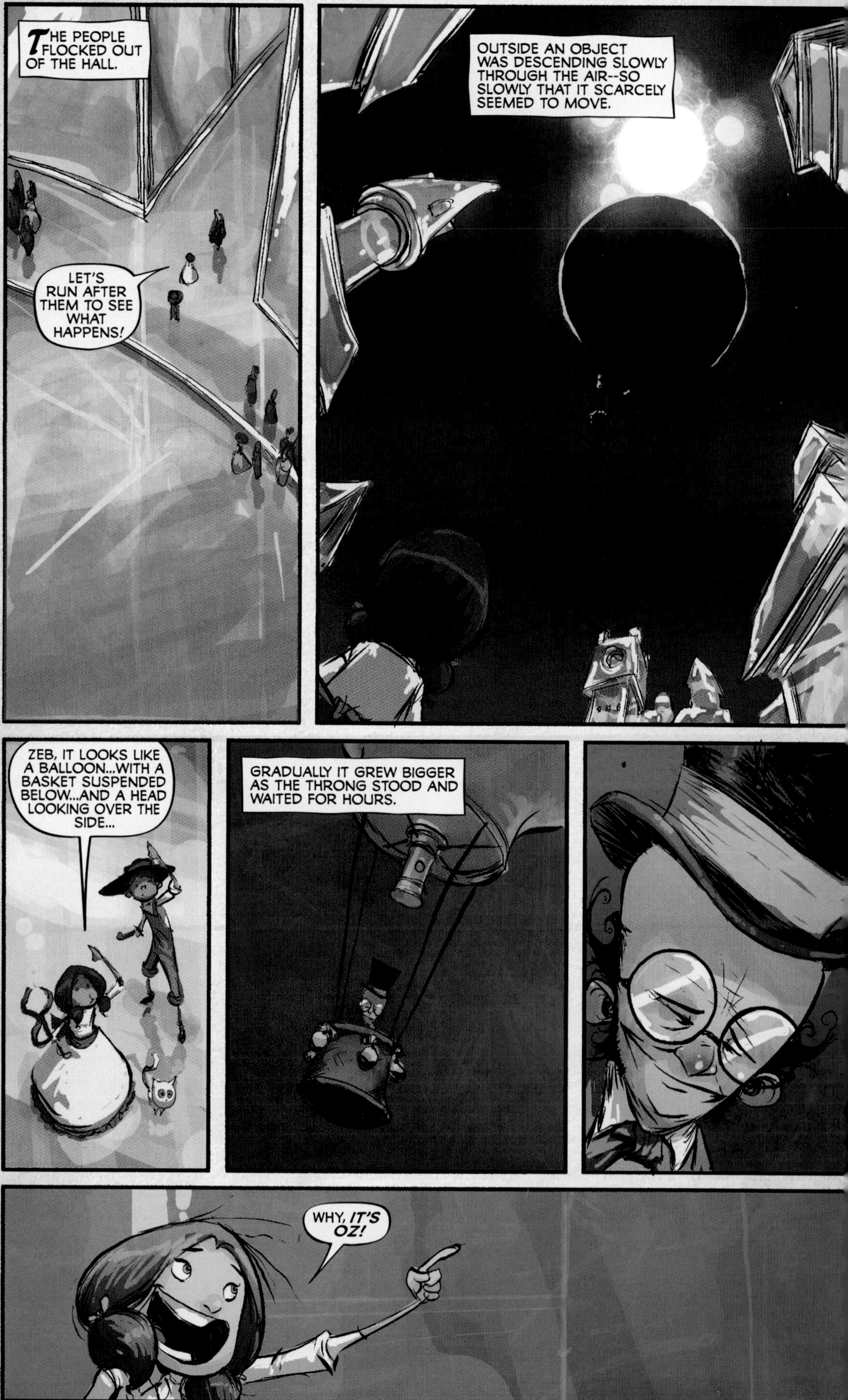
THE PEOPLE FLOCKED OUT OF THE HALL.
LET'S RUN AFTER THEM TO SEE WHAT HAPPENS!
OUTSIDE AN OBJECT WAS DESCENDING SLOWLY THROUGH THE AIR--SO SLOWLY THAT IT SCARCELY SEEMED TO MOVE.
ZEB, IT LOOKS LIKE A BALLOON...WITH A BASKET SUSPENDED BELOW...AND A HEAD LOOKING OVER THE SIDE...
GRADUALLY IT GREW BIGGER AS THE THRONG STOOD AND WAITED FOR HOURS.
WHY, *IT'S OZ!*